D0996953

ISBN 0.86112.939.3
© Brimax Books Ltd 1993. All rights reserved.
Published by Brimax Books Ltd, Newmarket, England CB8 7AU 1993.
Printed in France by Pollina, 85400 Luçon (France) - n° 14972

THE ADVENTURES OF
Bramble Bear

By Geoffrey Alan
Illustrated by Pamela Storey

BRIMAX BOOKS · NEWMARKET · ENGLAND

Bramble Bear

I wish I was...

"I do not want to be a bear today," sighs Bramble.
"I wish I was a bird. Then I could fly!"
He flaps his chubby little arms and runs down the hill, pretending to take off.
But he slips and roly-polies all the way to the bottom.
"Ohh!" he gasps, landing in thick grass.

"Now my head is buzzing!" he mutters. But then he sees a bee collecting pollen from a flower beside him.
"So you are making that buzzing noise!" grins Bramble. "Your black and yellow stripes are very smart. If I were a bee, I would make as much honey as possible!"

As the bee flies off, Bramble chases it until it enters a hollow tree-stump.
"Is that where you hide your honey?" asks Bramble.
"I'm sure you will not miss just a little bit."
Bramble pushes his paw into the tree. But he pulls it out very quickly. There are lots of bees in there. Now they are cross. They chase Bramble.

Bramble rushes towards
a waterfall. He hurries
underneath it. SPLASH!
Water pours all over him but
he stays there until, at last,
all the bees fly away.
Poor Bramble steps out. He
sits in the sun to dry his fur.
"I'm glad I'm not a bee,"
he nods. "They get very
cross indeed!"

Just then, something hops on to Bramble's tummy.

"A frog!" he smiles. "That's what I want to be. Hopping looks fun!"

The frog hops down and Bramble begins hopping, too. But he lands in some sticky mud. SPLOP!

"Oo . . . er!" he frowns. "Being a frog is very messy!"

Next moment, Bramble feels
something hit his head.
"Sorry!" calls a squirrel.
"I dropped the nut I was eating.
I will go and get another one."
Bramble gasps, amazed, as
he sees the squirrel leap from
branch to branch.
"If I were a squirrel, I could do
that!" he dreams.

"Wait for me!" calls Bramble, beginning to climb the tree. He follows the squirrel along a branch. But Bramble is too heavy and the branch starts to bend.

Bramble looks down and feels dizzy. The ground seems a long way down. Suddenly, the branch breaks and Bramble falls into some big, leafy ferns.

"Trees are very high things," Bramble says, looking up at the tree. "I'm glad I'm not a squirrel. I prefer being on the ground."

"Sssso do I," hisses a snake, slithering past.

Bramble lies on his tummy and tries to wriggle, too. But he cannot move from the same spot. "I couldn't be a snake," he puffs. "I would never get anywhere!"

"Let me help you," says a deer, towering over Bramble. "Hold on to my antlers." The deer pulls Bramble to his feet.

"Thank you," replies Bramble. "Your antlers are useful. I wish I had some."

Bramble finds two branches and holds them to his head. 'Now I have antlers, too!' he thinks.

Bramble trots along. But his antlers catch on a bush.

Bramble pulls and pushes, heaves and huffs to free the branch. Next moment, he falls into the bush. Poor Bramble completely disappears. Slowly, he clambers out again. "I don't think I want antlers, after all," says Bramble. "They get hooked on to things!"

"Bramble! BRAMBLE!"
he hears his Mother call.
"Coming!" he says, brushing
bits of leaf from his fur.
Bramble's Mother is waiting
on the doorstep, wiping her
paws on her apron. When she
sees Bramble, she shakes
her head.
"What a mess you look!
What have you been doing?"
she asks.

Indoors, Bramble explains while his Mother dries him after a bath.
"I was playing being other animals," he sighs. He tells his Mother everything that has happened to him.
She smiles and brushes his fur. "Your thick fur helped to save you from being stung by the bees," she says, "and from hurting yourself when you fell."

31

"It also stopped you getting scratched and catching a cold as it dries quickly," she adds. In no time, Bramble is the cleanest bear again. He sniffs freshly baked honey-cake. "Mm! I'm pleased I'm me, after all," he tells his Mother. "I have decided, I like being a bear!"

Say these words again

wriggle	fly
antler	stripes
hooked	honey
doorstep	shivers
thick	sticky
sniffs	dreams
hollow	branch

34

Who can you see . . .

squirrel

deer

frog

snake

Mother

Bramble Bear

The Missing Necklace

It is Bramble Bear's bedtime.
He pulls on his pyjamas and
slippers, then strolls into the
sitting room.
"Goodnight," he says, yawning.
But there is no reply. He sees
his father sitting in a chair, his
face hidden behind a big book.
"'Detective Stories'," mutters
Bramble, looking at the cover.

"Father, what does a detective do?" Bramble asks. His father puts down the book and answers. "He hunts for clues and solves mysteries." "Wow!" says Bramble. "That sounds exciting. But is it hard?" "Not always," grins his father. "I mean, I can see you have been in the cookie jar!" Bramble gasps.

"How did you know?" asks Bramble.

"Because you have crumbs on your chin and pyjamas," chuckles his father.

"Mother did say I could have a cookie before I went to bed, as long as I brush my teeth," Bramble explains quickly.

"I wish I were a detective!" That night, he dreams he is.

Next morning, when he wakes up, the sun is shining through his window.
Bramble dresses and hurries downstairs to see his father.
"He has gone out," says Bramble's mother.
"Can I borrow his magnifying glass?" asks Bramble. "The one he uses to look at his stamps."

"You must be very careful," Bramble's mother finally agrees. "Why do you want it?" "Detectives always have them," says Bramble, "and that is what I am going to be!" He sets off down the path but stops to peer through the magnifying glass at a spider. Bramble jumps. He forgets how big the special glass makes things seem!

"Now to search for clues,"
he thinks, walking on again.
Suddenly, he sees some
enormous, strange footprints.
Bramble looks at them again,
this time without his magnifying
glass.
"They really are huge!" he
mutters, in amazement.
"Whatever could have made
them? It's a mystery and I'm
just the bear to solve it!"

Bramble thinks for a minute, then shivers.
"Perhaps it is a monster frog!" Bravely, Bramble decides to find out. "That is what a real detective would do," he tells himself.
Bramble follows the tracks down to the river. They lead right into the water.

Bramble tiptoes on to the old wooden bridge.

"If it is a monster frog, I will soon see. I shall just wait here quietly," he thinks.

But no sooner does he glance down at the river, than lots of bubbles rise to the surface.

Bramble hears an odd gurgling sound below him.

Next moment, a figure appears. Poor Bramble is so surprised, he steps back and stumbles.

Only then does he notice something sparkle in the sunlight. Before he can look closer, he hears his father call, "Are you all right?"

"I think so," Bramble replies, sitting up. "I thought you were a monster frog!"

"Hardly!" laughs his father. "But I have been diving." He climbs up on to the riverbank and pulls off his goggles. Bramble sees he is wearing flippers.

"So they made those strange tracks," he frowns.

"Your mother lost her necklace here," explains his father. Bramble gasps. "That must be what I saw shining!"

"Here it is!" cries Bramble.
"Mother's necklace didn't fall in
the water. Look! It's hooked on
to the bottom of the bridge!"
"Well done, son," chuckles
Bramble's father. "However did
you know?"
"Oh, clues, I suppose," begins
Bramble. Then he grins,
"Or just good luck, really."

"What a clever detective you are!" smiles Bramble's mother, when he gives her the necklace. She puts it on, straight away. "I hope you did not mind me using your magnifying glass?" says Bramble to his father. "You can keep it," replies his father. "A detective always needs one!"

"That is very kind of you, Dad," says Bramble. "But I don't think I want to be a detective any more." "Why ever not?" asks Bramble's father as Bramble gives him back the magnifying glass.

"Well," begins Bramble, shuffling his feet, "if I had seen a monster frog, I would have been really frightened!"

Say these words again

hidden

clues

crumbs

borrow

teeth

goggles

monster

bubbles

sparkle

flippers

wait

detective

cookie

stumble

What can you see . . . .

magnifying glass

spider

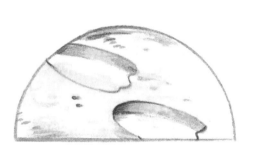

footprints

bridge

flippers

necklace

Bramble Bear
Pretends to be...

One morning, Bramble goes shopping with his mother. They see a big crowd. Everyone is very excited. They are clapping and taking photographs. "What is happening?" asks Bramble.

"Bradley Bear, the singer, is opening the new supermarket," says his mother. "He is very famous!" Afterwards, Bradley says hello to everyone.

"Being famous is great!"
thinks Bramble, on the way
home. "I would like to be
famous, so that everyone can
make a fuss of me!" He thinks
for a while.

"I know!" says Bramble.
"I will become a singer!"
He hurries indoors to fetch his
old toy guitar. He borrows his
mother's sunglasses, too.

Next, Bramble pulls out a plank from behind the shed. He stands it on two upturned buckets to make a stage. Stepping on to it, he strums his guitar and starts to sing and dance wildly. But the plank and buckets wobble.

"Help!" shouts Bramble, toppling off.

Betsy Bear from next door
comes to Bramble's rescue.
"What were you doing?" she
asks, helping him up.
"Oh . . . er . . . nothing
important," he replies, feeling
very silly. He is pleased to see
his mother's sunglasses are
not broken.
"No harm done," Bramble adds.
"You were lucky," smiles
Betsy. "You really went flying!"

"Flying! Yes, of course!" cries Bramble. "That's how to become famous!"
Soon he builds some big wings. Then he tells Betsy to fetch her friends to see The Famous Flying Bear!
At the top of a hill, Bramble fixes on his wings. But as he looks down the valley, he feels dizzy.
"I won't fly too high," he says.

A sudden gust of wind catches his wings and blows Bramble round and round. He spins into one of Betsy's friends, who is eating a chocolate-coated ice-cream.

Bramble's wings break and, SPLAT!, the ice-cream lands all over him.

"All flights today are off!" he says.

"Just look at you. What a mess!" says Bramble's mother, when he gets home. "Go and change at once!"

"Yes, I'm sorry," sighs Bramble.

Later, he sees his mother has washed all his dirty clothes and is hanging them to dry.

Bramble stares at the washing line for a moment and has another idea.

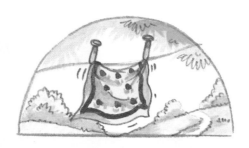

He finds a large sheet of paper and writes on it. 'See Bramble, the famous tight-rope walker', it says.

He pins it to a tree in the lane, beyond the garden.

"Roll up! ROLL UP!" he calls. Before long, lots of Bramble's friends gather to watch.

The young bear climbs some step-ladders to reach the washing line. In one paw, he holds a long garden cane. "Tight-rope walkers have a stick to help them balance," thinks Bramble, nervously. But no sooner does he step on the washing line than he slips. Everyone gasps!
Bramble disappears!

85

"Where is he?" cries Betsy. Then someone points to a bulging pillow case pegged to the line. Bramble has fallen into it.

"At least you had a nice, soft landing," laugh some rabbits as they pull him out.

Bramble turns very red and feels more silly than ever.

"I'm going to try something else," he mutters.

Next day, Bramble walks to the river. He stands on the dock and calls, "See Bramble, the famous bear, row to the other bank in record time!" A crowd soon lines the riverbank. Betsy is there, too. "Start the clock!" calls Bramble, climbing into his father's rowing boat. As he pulls hard on the oars, he hears lots of voices.

"They are cheering," decides Bramble. "I am famous, at last!"

Suddenly, he realises everyone is laughing. And no wonder! His boat is not moving at all. Bramble's father arrives and others help him pull in the boat's mooring line.

"Just as well you forgot to untie it, Bramble," says his father, sternly.

"I give up!" sighs Bramble. "I'll never be famous!"

"You already are!" smiles Betsy. "There is not another bear in the whole, wide world who gets up to all the things you do."

Everyone agrees and laughs again. This time, Bramble laughs with them.

"Er . . . would anyone like my autograph?" he asks.

Say these words again

photographs garden
famous balance
shed soft
silly river
wings mooring
ice cream laughs
dirty row

What can you see . . .

sunglasses

guitar

bucket

washing line

pillow case

boat

95

Bramble Bear

Can I help?

"Can I help?" Bramble asks his mother, who is having a baking morning in the kitchen.
"Yes, please," she smiles.
"Fetch me the flour from the cupboard. Then you can wash up for me."
Bramble reaches for the big bag of flour. But it is much heavier than he thinks.

He drops it. WHUMP! Flour bursts out everywhere in a dusty, white cloud. Bramble is covered in flour, too. Now he is a very white bear.

"I'm sorry," he sighs. "I was only trying to be helpful."

"You have given me more work," says Bramble's mother. "Now I will have to clean everything – including you!" Bramble has to change. Afterwards, he goes into the garden, where his father is digging.
"Can I help?" he asks.

"You could dig up some weeds for me," puffs his father. He stretches his back, then rubs it. "You know which are weeds, don't you?"

"Yes," Bramble nods. "Just leave it to me!"

"Very well," replies Bramble's father. "I will go indoors for a cup of coffee."

"Now I will show father just how helpful I can be," grins Bramble. He picks up the garden fork and begins to dig. Soon the wheelbarrow is full.
"I've finished!" Bramble calls.
"I will come and have a look," replies his father.
But when he walks into the garden, he stops and stares.
"Oh, no!"

"You have dug up my prize flowers!" groans Bramble's father.

"B . . .but I thought they were weeds," says Bramble, quietly. Bramble's father takes the garden fork and starts to lift things out of the wheelbarrow with it.

"I will have to plant all these again," he says.

Bramble goes to his bedroom.
"I think I will be helping most if I keep out of the way," he mutters.
As he looks around the room, he remembers what his mother is always saying; "Bramble, your room is in such a mess."
"I know!" cries Bramble.
"I will tidy my room. That will please mother."

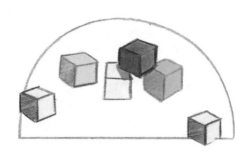

Bramble begins by picking up his clothes and putting them in the wardrobe. He even folds them neatly first. Shortly, all his toys are packed in a wooden chest.

"That leaves the books," says Bramble.

There are lots of books scattered under his bed.

Bramble picks them up and goes to put them on the shelf. But he holds too many at once. He drops some and tries to catch them.

Bramble loses his balance and falls back on to his bed.

CRASH! the bed collapses. Bramble is not hurt. But his mother and father come rushing in.

"Don't tell me!" groans his mother. "You were trying to help again."

"I will have to mend the bed," frowns his father.

Bramble decides to be really helpful and go for a walk. He has not gone far when he sees two young rabbits pointing up at a tree.

"Our kite is stuck on that branch," they tell Bramble. "I will climb up and get it for you," he says, eagerly. Carefully, he climbs up and gets closer to the kite. He pulls himself farther and farther along the branch. The kite is hooked on the very end of it.

"I can't quite reach the kite," thinks Bramble. So he shakes the branch and the kite falls down.

"Thank you. *Thank you*," call the rabbits happily.

"Glad to be of help," says Bramble. Then he mutters under his breath, "At last!"

The two rabbits run off, pulling their kite on a string. Bramble grins. "Just wait until I tell mother and father."
He starts to climb down. But he cannot turn around!
"I'm stuck!" he groans. He calls the rabbits back and they fetch his father, with a ladder.
"So much for being a helpful bear. Now I'm the one who needs help!"

Say these words again

morning	chest
flour	shelf
garden	mend
weeds	kite
stares	branch
prize	string
mess	ladder

What are they doing?

baking

digging

folding

lifting

pointing

climbing